THE

DANGEROUS

JOURNEY

OF SHERMAN THE SHEEP

I am the Good Shepherd. The Good Shepherd lays down his life for the sheep. I gave them eternal life, and they shall never perish. Neither shall anyone snatch them out of my hand.

~ Jesus of Nazareth
John 10:11,28

THE
DANGEROUS
JOURNEY
OF SHERMAN THE SHEEP

∾

BY DEAN DAVIS

CLADACH
Publishing

Published with worldwide English rights by

CLADACH Publishing
PO Box 336144
Greeley, CO 80633
WWW.CLADACH.com

Printed and bound in Canada

Cover: photo of flock of sheep in the Cevenne
mountains, France, by David Lawton; photo of
young sheep by Larry Lawton

Library Of Congress Control Number: 2005926709

ISBN-13: 978-0-975961-92-6
ISBN-10: 0-975961-92-6

CONTENTS

1
LIFE in the FOLD

Sherman the sheep lived with his father, Bertram, his mother, Eunice, and his Uncle Billy in a far-away land called God's Country. Have you ever been there? If so, then you know that it's a rugged place, where life is seldom easy. Yet Sherman and his family were really quite content. In fact, they considered themselves blessed — for they all belonged to the little flock of the Good Shepherd.

Let me tell you a little about their life together.

Each spring, in the time of the wildflowers and the turtledoves, the Shepherd left His Father's house and took the family flock to the high country. Their destination was a lonely valley deep in the hills and an ancient sheepfold with four high walls of stone. This became their home away from home, the place where all their journeys began and ended.

Early in the year, when grass was plentiful, their travels were short, hardly more than outings. At dawn the Shepherd would open the gate of the fold, whistle for the sheep, and lead His flock to a nearby meadow with a pool of fresh spring water to drink. Then at dusk they would all return to the safety of the fold's strong walls.

But as spring gave way to summer, and summer to fall, the journeys grew longer and more difficult. They'd be gone for many days, camping beneath the stars or in caves. The meadows grew fewer and the water more scarce—and to find them the flock had often to follow their Shepherd through dark, narrow canyons, where wolves or lions might be lurking in the shadows.

Yes, this was the dangerous time of year, a time when sheep could get hungry, thirsty, or even hurt. Needless to say, the Shepherd took such dangers very seriously. But as for the sheep, they simply trusted in their Master's care. They knew that sooner or later He would give them rest, just as He always had.

And as for Sherman—well, for him danger was just another word for adventure; and adventure was the one thing Sherman loved best!

Here, then, was how they lived—ever journeying through a land both rich and barren, beautiful and deadly. The older sheep stayed close by the Shepherd's side, while the younger ones frolicked to the left and right. But all knew their Master's voice and all followed Him wherever He went. They knew He cared for them, and they were very glad to belong to Him.

2
CURIOUS SHERMAN

Late one fall afternoon as the sheep began to gather around the Shepherd (at evening-time He would play His harp and sing for them), Bertram suddenly missed Sherman. He raised himself up on his hind legs, leaned against the trunk of a nearby tree, and looked around in a big circle.

"Hmm," said Bertram, searching the flock. "He's not grazing with his brothers, and he's not playing with the lambs." Then he saw him. On the far side of the meadow, in the shadows of a thick grove of trees, Sherman was talking with some strangers.

Now to understand what was happening, you need to know more about Sherman. Among the "little ones" of the flock, he was the oldest. Until recently this had posed no problem. He'd been content to eat and play with the other lambs who loved him and regarded him as their leader.

Lately, though, he had grown strangely restless. The lambs' games were not as fun. Their explorations grew stale and routine. The company of the little ones was somehow not enough. For Sherman, it was all quite puzzling. But his father Bertram understood very well: unlike his younger friends, Sherman the sheep was a lamb no more.

Bertram hoped that those young rams across the meadow could be true friends to his son. But his heart warned him to be careful. Over the years Bertram had learned much about strangers. He had

found that few of them loved the ways of the Good
Shepherd. Usually, they preferred their own ways—
ways that seemed new and exciting, but which in
fact could get a young ram in big trouble.

Pondering these things, Bertram made a decision.
He would go to the grove and introduce himself to
Sherman's new friends. He would get acquainted
with them and find out more about them. *Perhaps*, he
thought, *they will be just the companions my son needs.*

Feeling good about his plan, Bertram set out
across the meadow. Soon, however, he noticed
something happening, something disappointing.
One by one the young rams were nodding "good-
bye" to his son and heading for a large flock camped
in the distance. Bertram wondered, *Have they seen
me? Are they slipping away because of me? If so, why?*

When Bertram finally reached the grove,

Sherman was alone. For a long time Bertram stood silently behind his son, who was gazing through the shadows towards the strangers' flock. Just behind that flock there rose a huge, dark mountain. Sherman stared, having no idea his father stood near.

Looking at the distant, looming mountain, Bertram realized that his fears were well-founded. A sad, worried look crept across his face. Then, as quietly as he could, he spoke.

"So here you are."

Sherman jumped and spun around. "Father! I didn't know you were here!"

"Sorry to startle you, Son. But it was time for the campfire, and we couldn't find you anywhere."

Sherman glanced about nervously. He fumbled for words. "Oh, well, if you don't mind, I think I'll skip the campfire tonight." He stared at his hoofs.

Sherman's words pierced his father's heart. After a long pause Bertram asked, "What were those young rams saying to you, Sherman? I'm curious to know what could keep you from the evening music you've always loved."

"Oh, nothing … nothing special, I mean," answered Sherman, who still could not look his father in the eyes. Then he lifted his head. With a trace of impatience in his voice, he said, "Father, there's nothing wrong with them. They're just some rams I met this morning and we started talking—"

"I didn't say there was anything wrong with them, Son. But tell me, did they speak to you about that mountain?"

"The mountain?" asked Sherman nervously.

"Yes, Sin Mountain. Did they speak to you about Sin Mountain?"

"They didn't say anything about any *Sin* Mountain, Father." Sherman turned his head and looked across the barren field towards the strangers' flock. "But they did tell me about their flock, and about *Pleasure* Mountain, where their shepherds pasture them nearly all the time."

At the sound of these words Bertram stood very still and said nothing at all. He considered carefully the crucial words he knew he must now speak.

"Well, have any of your new friends ever been up on this 'Pleasure Mountain'?"

"Oh yes, they all have. Some of them have gone up quite a ways!" Sherman could not conceal his excitement.

"And did they enjoy it?"

"They said it was fantastic," replied Sherman triumphantly.

"I see. And now that they've been up there, are they happy?"

"Happy?"

"Yes, happy—content, at rest in their hearts?"

"Father, they're more than happy, they're excited! They can't wait to go back up there. Only, next time they want to go up even farther!"

Bertram thought for a moment. "It sounds to me like they feel the need to keep going back, farther and farther up. Am I right?"

The question irritated Sherman. "Father, I don't know what they feel they need. All I know is that they *want* to go back. They're excited about it."

"It seems they told you quite a bit about the mountain," observed Bertram.

"Well, to be honest Father, that's pretty much all they talked about."

"Then let me ask you something, Sherman. Was there any room for God in their thoughts? Did they speak at all about God, as we do in our flock?"

Sherman wished he could say "yes." But since he couldn't, he just stood there in silence.

After an uncomfortable moment, Bertram spoke again. "One more question, Sherman, and then I'll go back to the campfire. Did any of your new friends ever reach the top of that mountain?"

Sherman reflected for a moment. "No, I don't think so. But that's what they're all trying to do."

"Did any of their friends ever reach it?"

A strange uneasiness came over Sherman and he answered, "Well, no. One almost did."

"And what became of him?"

"Nobody knows. I guess he's still up on the mountain. He hasn't come back yet."

Bertram took a step or two towards his son, and looked intently into his eyes. "I will tell you why that sheep hasn't come home, Sherman. Only remember, these are not my words but the words of our Shepherd, who cannot lie.

"The true name of that place is Sin Mountain, for all that is seen and done there is displeasing to God. Your friends call it Pleasure Mountain. Sad to say, that is partly true. Those who climb it do find pleasure … for a while. But your friends didn't tell you that the pleasures soon fade away, leaving only guilt and shame. And they didn't tell you that such pleasures leave a restless craving for more pleasure. That's why they want to go higher and higher on the mountain: they think they'll find satisfaction at the top. But they never will. Shall I tell you why?"

Sherman didn't want to hear the answer, but he

nodded "yes" anyway.

"It's because our enemies live up there, enemies you've never seen and can barely imagine. And they have just one purpose — to steal, kill, and destroy."

Bertram took another step forward. Then he spoke from the very depths of his heart. "Many sheep have tried to reach the top, Sherman. But long before they ever did, they found their enemies waiting for them. Believe me, Son, the only thing you'll discover on the heights of Sin Mountain is trouble. Big trouble. Maybe even death."

With these words an awkward silence fell upon them both. Sherman dared not speak. His father had nothing more to say.

The sun had set. The twilight was fast dwindling. And now, through the cool night air, they could hear the faint but lovely sound of the Shepherd's music.

Looking across the field, they saw the light of a fire and the Shepherd seated on a rock, with all the flock gathered round.

"The singing has begun, Sherman. Let's join them." With that, Bertram turned and walked towards the light.

Sherman watched his father go. He looked again at the fire, imagining the smiles on every face. He remembered how just yesterday he had been among them. Yes, he had to admit that the campfires were fun. But now he had met new friends and learned about new kinds of fun. A whole new world was opening up before him. With pictures of Pleasure Mountain filling his mind, the former joys of the campfire just seemed (Sherman felt bad about thinking this) well … boring; boring and even downright *lambish*.

As soon as Bertram realized that Sherman was not following, he turned around and looked at his son. Light from the fire twinkled in Sherman's eyes, and draped his fluffy coat with hues of gold. How handsome he looked! But there, rising threateningly behind him, was the great, tempting form of Sin Mountain.

If only Sherman knew the dangers of that mountain! Bertram was angry—angry with those foolish young rams and their careless shepherds and the evil mountain where they camped. But mostly he was sad. Why was there so much evil and danger in this world? Why must his son learn of these things, and why must he learn to fear them all his life? Tears gathered in Bertram's eyes.

"Sherman, the time has come for you to choose for yourself whether you will come to the fire. But you need to understand this: In the end, you really have only two choices." Bertram looked longingly at the fire. "You can choose the Shepherd's way." Then he turned sadly toward the mountain. "Or you can choose the way of our enemies."

The old ram sighed wearily. "That's the hardest part of being an adult, Sherman: choosing—all the time choosing." Then, after a short pause, he suddenly straightened his head, looked sternly at his son and said, "But that's the way the Lord has arranged it, and He never makes a mistake. Now, I'm going to the campfire; and you, young ram, are going to bed. And one last thing: Don't go near that mountain!"

Bertram turned and trotted briskly back to the flock. And Sherman, sullenly dragging his hoofs, went to bed.

3
DANGEROUS DECISION

Long after the rest of the flock had retired for the night, Sherman lay wide awake. The moon had come up, and in its milky light the distant mountain glowed eerily. Sherman stared at it as he thought about today's meeting with his new friends.

How he wanted to be like them, so grown up, so independent, so knowledgeable! And how curious he was about the secret adventures they'd discussed in whispers among themselves.

Sherman, wanting to fit in, had tried telling them about his adventures with the Good Shepherd—how

He had rescued the flock from lions, sheltered them in caves, and pastured them in hidden mountain valleys which neither man nor ram had ever seen before. But they just laughed at him as though he were a silly lamb, then went on talking about the pleasures of "The Mountain." Poor Sherman! What did he know about all that? He felt totally left out.

So, after much thought, Sherman decided there was only one way to win their respect. It was a bold plan—and, in his humble opinion, a shrewd one. Now all he had to do was persuade himself that it was right.

"Father has his own friends, so why can't I have mine? All day long, nothing but lambs, lambs, lambs follow me around everywhere I go! I'm sick of them." Sherman chose to forget how much fun he always had playing with the lambs, and how important it made him feel when they looked up to him as their leader.

"And all that talk about 'Sin Mountain' and 'displeasing God' and 'meeting our enemies.' I bet Father just wants to scare me so I'll stay around this boring old flock all the time."

But once again Sherman was only fooling himself. For life with the Good Shepherd was actually quite full of adventure, as he himself had tried to tell the strangers. Yes, things got dreary from time to time, but even then there were many simple pleasures to enjoy — daily food, close friends, gatherings around the campfire, and fearless rest under the Shepherd's watchful eye. But, beneath the shadow of Sin Mountain, Sherman had somehow forgotten these things as well.

"Anyway," said Sherman aloud to himself,

triumphantly concluding his train of thought, "I'll just go up the mountain one time. Surely there's no harm in that. The flock will spend the day grazing, so Father won't expect to see me till evening. And if I could just make it to the top ... why, then those guys would *have* to let me be their friend!"

Sherman had made up his mind. And though a still, small voice deep in his heart warned him against making this decision, Sherman rose bravely to his feet. "Silly fears," he said to himself. "A young ram has got to have friends. Surely the Lord wants a ram to have friends."

And having thus convinced himself, Sherman the sheep slipped quietly away from the flock, and headed through the darkness for Sin Mountain.

4
UP THE MOUNTAIN

It was still dark when Sherman reached the foot of the mountain, though the eastern horizon now grew pale with the coming dawn. The walk had been more difficult than Sherman expected. Groping in the darkness, he had stumbled and fallen several times. At one point he lost his bearings and wandered too near his friends' flock. The dogs heard him and barked loudly. Had it not been for a strong night wind, they would surely have caught his scent — and Sherman, too!

But now, resting at the foot of the mountain, he watched in awe as the huge greenish-brown form emerged from the shadows in the growing light. Sherman soon forgot the perils of the previous night, as his mind filled with visions of conquest.

"*That* doesn't look so big," said Sherman. And to a self-confident, inexperienced sheep, it really didn't.

"And what did Father mean, saying our enemies live up on top? The top is completely barren. Why, nothing could live up there!"

Now this was not quite true. The upper slopes were indeed rocky and barren, but the top itself was covered by a thick, grey cloud. All Sherman could really see was the cloud—and a few birds (he thought they were eagles) flying in and out of it. Sherman assumed the terrain beneath the cloud was rocky, barren and lifeless, like all the rest. But—as he would soon find out—his assumption was wrong … dangerously wrong.

"Father must have been thinking about some other mountain," he happily concluded. "No enemies up there!" Emboldened by his own words, he eagerly arose and headed out for the beckoning slopes nearby.

It wasn't long before Sherman spotted a wide, well-worn trail leading upwards to the top. Though he saw no one else, he was comforted to realize how many other sheep had gone before him.

"If it was really dangerous," he reasoned, "folks would have found out by now! There would be signs and everything! Boy, Father was sure wrong this time!"

This conclusion left Sherman feeling positively chipper, so much so that he stepped up his pace and danced up the trail. It wasn't long, however, before he saw before him a thick forest. And what he found there slowed him down soon enough.

"There's something funny about this place," said a puzzled Sherman, shortly after entering the shadowed woods. Looking around pensively, he tried to determine just what it was that made him feel so odd. Then it struck him. The forest was completely silent ... silent and still. There were no signs of animal life anywhere—no birds, no squirrels, no rabbits or foxes—not even insects!

Now that's strange, thought Sherman. *Not a single critter. Oh well, maybe it's too early. When the sun's farther up, I bet I'll see some animals.*

Unfortunately for Sherman's theory, the sun had long since risen, as Sherman could easily have seen from the thin shafts of light filtering down through the tangled trees. It was, however, a light he preferred to ignore.

As Sherman pressed more deeply into the woods, he noticed that the shapes of the trees were changing. Yes, it was just as his friends had said. Down in the plains, the trees stood tall and strong like cedars or bushy and playful like myrtles. But here they grew like corkscrews — low, bent and twisted, as if struggling painfully against some invisible force pulling them down to the ground. They were impressive all right, just as the rams had told him. But the impression left on Sherman by the grotesque trees was not one of excitement. No, he felt sorry for the trees and wished he could somehow help them.

"Get ahold of yourself, ram," said Sherman. "Trees can't feel pain." But the more he looked at their twisted trunks, the more compassion he felt. So as Sherman trotted on, he tried to keep his thoughts on his mission and his eyes to the ground.

The strategy worked well. Soon he emerged from the dark wood and caught a fresh view of the clouded peak above. It was twice as big and twice as near (or so it seemed)! A surge of optimism coursed through his body, scattering every trace of gloom.

Excited, Sherman surveyed the great slopes ahead. He could see that the upward trail circled the mountain several times. It would not be an easy climb. "But," he declared aloud, "I can make it by noon. No food and no rests. Just keep on going, and I *will* make it by noon!"

And thus resolved, he set off eagerly on the next leg of the journey.

Sherman had, of course, every intention of sticking to his plan. But after little more than an hour of difficult climbing, even his most fervent intentions began yielding to a persistent knot that was forming in the pit of his stomach. Sherman was getting hungry.

His pace began to slow, and his eyes began to wander. The mountain, which from below had looked so lush and appealing, offered no help. *There's gotta be some food out there somewhere*, thought Sherman. But wherever he looked, he saw only scrubby green bushes covering the drab slopes as far as the eye could see.

As Sherman pressed on, however, he began to notice on some of the bushes an occasional cluster of berries. At first, he paid them scant attention, figuring they were too few, too small, and too tough to reach. But as he went farther, the clusters increased, and the bright red berries seemed to beckon him to turn aside. *Well*, reasoned Sherman, casting a backward glance down the mountain, *I've come pretty far pretty fast. Maybe a little break wouldn't hurt.* How wrong he was.

Sherman left the trail and approached one of the bushes. It was loaded with big bunches of berries, inside and out. Cautiously, he reached his mouth around a tiny cluster, bit off three or four berries, and chewed slowly.

"Hmmmm," said Sherman, "not bad." The berries were hard, but when pressed between his teeth they released a thick, sweet syrup that flowed like honey down his throat.

"Not bad at all," he said, eating a second, larger cluster. The second led to a third, and the third to a fourth.

"Ram alive!" exclaimed the enthusiastic convert, beginning to feast on the bigger bunches, "these things are great!"

And great they were—to the taste. But had Sherman been a little more observant, he would have noticed that, unlike the food the Shepherd gave him, the berries did nothing to relieve his hunger.

In fact, had you been there to watch, you might have thought he was getting more hungry, rather than less. For, to put it mildly, Sherman was quickly forgetting his manners. No sooner would he swallow one bite, than he would attack the bush for another. Alas, it wasn't long before he was gulping, grunting, and even groveling beneath the bush. This was not the Sherman his parents had raised, nor was this a Sherman his parents would ever want to see.

"Ow!" cried Sherman, coming upon an unexpected obstacle. Having eaten all the berries on the outside of the bush, he was now going for the smaller ones deep inside. But much to his surprise,

the berries on the inner branches were protected
by sharp thorns. And no nose—however clever or
determined—could avoid them.

"Owwwwww!" he screamed again, this time
louder. "You stupid thorns—get outta my way!"

Poor Sherman! When he angrily thrust his face
in again, the uncooperative thorns refused to budge.
An agonized yowl echoed across the mountain, as
the crazed ram violently tore his wounded nose
from the branches.

If only he could have stopped! But Sherman's
uncontrollable desire for the strange berries was
now much stronger than his common sense, stronger
even than his fear of pain. So, for the sake of a
few berries, Sherman kept wounding himself on the
thorns, over and over and over again.

In the end, however, the pain won out. Sherman

finally got the message that his mouth, his nose, even his eyes, were now in real danger. In a sudden panic, he tore himself from the bush, leaped onto the path and ran up the mountain for dear life.

It was not a pretty sight, our fine young friend with a bloody face, cursing and screaming at the top of his voice, "You stupid thorns—I hate you, I HATE YOU!" But at least he was free. And in days ahead he would learn to be grateful for the "stupid thorns." If they had not stopped him from devouring berries, he might well have eaten himself to death.

Out on the open slopes again, and comforted by the warm morning sun, the shaky traveler slowly returned to his old, easy-going self.

"Ram-o-ram! The guys shoulda warned me about those berries," said Sherman, feeling slightly betrayed.

And so, striving to look on the bright side, Sherman pressed on, half hoping that his "adventures" on Pleasure Mountain were now over.

They definitely were not.

5
MORE SURPRISES

About two hours had gone by when Sherman rounded a curve and entered the shady back side of the mountain. There, not far ahead of him, he saw a huge, solitary tree. It looked like an oak, though the trunk and lower boughs were more twisted than those of any oak he'd ever seen. Its foliage was thick, so much so that Sherman could hardly see the upper branches. All around the tree was a bed of lush, green leaves — very inviting indeed to the weary traveler. But what intrigued Sherman most was a gaping crack in the ground that circled its trunk. Leaves from the tree kept falling into the crack. And out of it rose a pale yellow smoke, coiling and twisting through the air like fingers beckoning.

As he advanced to take a closer look, he again heard the little voice in his heart warning him to go no farther. But this strange new sight had aroused his curiosity. So Sherman persuaded himself that such misgivings were simply part of his great adventure into the unknown, and certainly not to be heeded fully. He decided to get close enough to examine the smoke while keeping a safe distance from the crack.

Then, as if it saw him coming, the thick column of smoke twisted its way towards Sherman. When it reached him, the smoke wrapped itself around him like a snake. A sweet, moldy smell filled not only Sherman's nostrils, but, somehow, his mind as well.

The more he inhaled, the more the world around him became like a dream. Sherman started laughing.

He spun himself around. Then he laughed louder and spun himself some more. "Hey, this stuff is neat!" he exclaimed. Wanting more of it, Sherman now began to follow the smoke wherever it led. He did not notice, however, that it was drawing him closer and closer to the crack.

Sherman's mood changed. The world still looked like a dream, but now he felt that he had great power over the dream, as if he were a mighty magician who could do anything he wished with a wave of his hand. Suddenly, a daring challenge entered his mind: *I wonder if I could leap over that crack.* In answer to the challenge, Sherman boasted to himself, "No problem! I can jump it easy!" Now in reality, the crack was over fifteen feet wide, and there was no way a sheep of any size could leap across it. But Sherman was not in reality. So he started to run.

How foolish he looked, this proud young ram who thought he was running so swiftly, but who was actually staggering and stumbling towards his death! Then, before he reached the edge, something peculiar happened, something that saved his life.

As Sherman surged ahead, the form of a man suddenly appeared before him, right in front of the crack. The man wore a shepherd's robe of rough white wool — whiter than the whitest white Sherman had ever seen. A thick club hung menacingly at his side, and in his right hand he held a tall, straight staff. His eyes — filled with anger and indignation — were steadfastly fixed upon Sherman's, striking terror into the poor sheep's soul. Even the smoke — which boiled all around the mysterious shepherd — seemed to cower and shrink back from his powerful presence.

Very deliberately, the man lifted his staff and held it across his chest, as if to block the progress of the oncoming ram. As soon as he did, Sherman's heart began to race and his head began to spin. Nausea and trembling seized his entire body. Helpless, Sherman closed his eyes, staggered forward once or twice, and collapsed to the ground. For a few seconds he just lay there, lost in the whirling darkness of his own mind and muttering to himself, "No problem, no problem at all." Then, after throwing up every berry in his stomach, he slipped into unconsciousness.

Sherman's second adventure on the Mountain had come to its pitiful end.

6
ONWARD!

The heat of the afternoon sun finally woke Sherman. Sluggishly he rose to his feet, shook his head, and tried to figure out where he was. Then, as if through a fog, the events of the morning came back to his mind.

First he remembered the crack. Sherman turned around to look. To his surprise, it was only eight or ten feet away (hardly the "safe distance" that Sherman had decided to keep from the crack). Since no smoke was coming out, he walked over to the edge and looked down. He found himself staring into thick darkness—he could see no bottom at all!

Instantly Sherman pulled back. "Yipes!" he cried. "Two more leaps and I'd have been a dead ram!"

Then Sherman remembered the form of the man who looked like a shepherd. Nervously he thought, *Must've been the smoke … made my mind play tricks on me*. But that didn't stop him from quickly looking around, just to make sure he really was alone. Then he looked again at the crack. If it was only a trick of his mind, then thank God for it. It had surely saved his life!

A shiver went through Sherman's aching body. Trembling with fear, he quickly turned, ran for the trail, and headed up the mountain once again.

As Sherman put some distance between himself and the tree, he began to mutter about what had happened there. "Ram! That place was … *weird*," observed Sherman cautiously, wishing he could say "fun," but knowing he couldn't.

Then he noticed something else: for some reason he felt dirty. The puzzled sheep glanced over his shoulder to look at his wool. "No," he said, "still white as usual." But outwardly white or not, he knew he wanted no one to see him now—especially not the Good Shepherd.

The more he pondered these things, the more Sherman wondered just why his friends had called this place "Pleasure Mountain." So far, the pleasures had been few and the fears and sorrows many. "Maybe I should just turn around and go home. … But then, how would I get those rams to be my friends?"

As Sherman was thus debating with himself, it suddenly dawned on him that he was feeling quite warm. He stopped and looked upwards. The sun stood high and hot in the sky. A wave of panic hit him. "What have I done?" he cried. "I was going to make the top by noon—and it's way past that already!"

Sherman's stomach flip-flopped. Somewhere deep in his heart he knew that this was his last chance. If he didn't go back now, his father would surely find out. But he'd come this far already. How could he give up now?

With a surge of determination, Sherman made his decision. "No," he declared, "I must reach the top. That's the only way to impress my new friends!"

So, picking up his pace yet again, the young sheep pressed on.

"And this time," he vowed, "no more distractions. There's no time to lose!"

7
ONE LITTLE PEEK

Sherman had meant what he said about no more distractions. And after his experience at the crack, he was more cautious than ever about "adventures" on Pleasure Mountain. Nevertheless, it wasn't long before something happened that almost caused him to break his vow.

As he once again rounded a curve leading onto the back side of the mountain, Sherman noticed another large oak tree in the distance. What's more, he also saw some sheep standing beside it. About thirty in number, they huddled together in a tight circle, looking down at something on the ground.

I wonder what they're looking at, thought Sherman.

Well, as you might imagine, the shaky, lonely traveler was much relieved to find some fellow sheep. Yet, after all he'd been through, he thought it wise to be careful: perhaps this tree was just as dangerous as the last!

So, before the others noticed him, the weary and wary Sherman hid himself behind a bush. From there he would assess the situation, and then decide whether to make his presence known.

From his hiding place, Sherman saw that most of the rams had gathered around a large pit and were staring into it. Something down there had captured their attention. Their bodies were frozen. Their eyes were wide and dull. Their mouths hung open. Occasionally one among them would rouse to life, point down, and crack a joke that made the others laugh.

Then they all lowered their heads again and stared in silence. *I wonder what they're all looking at*, thought Sherman again.

Despite a foul odor, which his nose told him was definitely coming from the pit, the rams kept crowding closer and closer to the edge.

Finally Sherman's curiosity got the better of him. *Whatever's down there*, he reasoned, *it doesn't seem to be hurting those guys. Surely there's no harm in a little peek*. So Sherman decided he would come out from behind his bush, greet the others, and then join them for a quick look.

But just before he moved he saw a small group of rams break away from the crowd. One of them, who seemed to be the leader, kept pausing and turning his head back and forth, as if he were looking for something. Then his face lit up.

"Hey Dudley!" cried the grinning leader. With his gang following him, he bounded toward a large rock in the near distance.

Surreptitiously looking in the same direction, Sherman noticed for the first time a small black sheep, who was nestled in the shade of the rock almost as if he were hiding. He was gazing at the sky, swaying his head from side to side, and moving his mouth rhythmically. "Why, he's singing!" exclaimed Sherman in an amazed whisper. And judging from the look of pleasure on the face of the black sheep, he was enjoying himself fully.

Sherman liked the little ram immediately and hoped he could get to know him. But something about this situation troubled Sherman. He decided to remain hidden a little longer. He would watch and learn what he could.

"Hey Dudley," yelled the leader as he approached the little black sheep. "Come on over and take a look!" With a crafty grin on his face, he winked at the rest of the gang. "This pit's fantastic—and it's educational, too!"

The gang whistled and hooted their agreement.

Dudley's smile had disappeared; even from a distance, Sherman saw fear flickering in his eyes. "No thanks, Nickey, you guys go ahead." Dudley rose nervously to his feet.

"What're ya doin', lookin' for birds again—or singin' one of yer stupid songs?" said another ram, the largest among them. His muscles were tensed and his voice dripped with disgust. Dudley's legs shook visibly beneath him, and his body started swaying like a boat on rolling seas.

"Come on, Lou, mellow out," said Nickey with

the same sly grin pasted across his face. "Maybe Dudley's just bein' shy. Maybe he's just sittin' over here trying to get up his courage to take a look."

"Fat chance," said Lou, glaring at Dudley. "This guy never wants to do the stuff we do. Why do ya keep lettin' him come with us, anyway?"

"Of course he wants to do the stuff we do!" exclaimed Nickey. "Tell him he's wrong, Dudley. Tell Lou you like being with us, and that you're gonna check out this pit right now. Go ahead—you tell him, Dudley."

At this point, Dudley slowly sank to the ground right before their feet. This seemed to please the rams, especially Lou.

"You know I like being with you guys," Dudley said, looking up nervously at Nickey. "I really do. It's just that some of the stuff we do makes me feel

… well, sort of funny. Not all of it, just some of it."

"Now Dudley, what's the use of bein' in a gang if we don't do stuff together?" said Nickey. "And besides, you've never seen this pit before. How can you *feel funny* about it already?"

"I've heard about it. I guess just hearing about it made me feel funny," explained Dudley.

Lou stood restlessly behind Nickey, scraping his hoofs on the ground like an angry bull.

"I don't know," said Nickey with an air of concern. "If you don't start joinin' in a little more, somebody around here's gonna get insulted. It's hard to say what might happen in a case like that. I think you'd better come with us to that pit … just for safety's sake." Now there was a menacing tone in Nickey's voice, too.

"Please," said the black sheep, "I'd rather not."

Nickey's face flushed with anger. He was obviously unaccustomed to being refused. In a controlled voice he said, "Well, now you've done it, Dudley. You've gone and insulted poor Lou here, and all the rest of us too." The sly smile returned to his face. "But I know you don't really mean it. You're just scared, just a little shy. So to help you out, I'm gonna let Lou escort you to the pit." Nickey stepped aside. Then Lou, with evident pleasure, stepped forward.

Dudley's eyes darted frantically, searching the face of every ram, looking for compassion and help. But he found none. Slowly he lowered his head in defeat. "That won't be necessary," he said softly. "I'll go by myself."

"Atta boy, Dudley! I knew you could do it!" Nickey was ecstatic.

"Atta boy, Dudley," echoed the rest of the gang,

laughing among themselves.

Dudley rose, and with his face to the ground he trudged slowly towards the pit. The gang followed close at his tail, cracking jokes and nudging him along. Lou scowled and brought up the rear.

Nickey shouted to the rams at the pit, "Hey you guys, here comes Dudley—he wants to take a look!"

"Yeah," said one of the gang. "Here comes the Dud!" The rams thought this was very funny, and all chanted in unison, "Here comes the Dud, here comes the Dud!"

When Dudley and the little gang arrived at the pit, Nickey motioned and the chanting stopped. Winking at everyone, he pretended to scold them.

"Now you guys should be ashamed of your-selves, makin' fun of my friend Dudley. This here is a very sensitive sheep who has lots of *funny feelings*.

Actually, we're quite honored to have him around. So you guys clear away, 'cuz Dudley is my personal guest at this pit."

Abruptly the cloud of sheep parted, making a narrow path that led to the edge of the pit. Nickey escorted Dudley to his place and remained at his right hoof. Lou, who had appointed himself Dudley's watch-guard, stationed himself at his left. Then all the rest found their places. In seconds, the entire pit was ringed with rams.

Still hiding behind his bush, Sherman had seen the fear in Dudley's eyes and the hatred in Lou's. He had heard the other rams chanting and making fun of the little black sheep. Sherman thought, *Why won't they let him sit by his rock and sing?*

Sherman was also troubled by the goings on at the pit. Whatever they were watching down there,

Dudley obviously didn't like it. Nickey would point in one direction, nudging Dudley with his left shoulder, trying to spark his interest. Then Lou would point in another direction, bumping him with his right shoulder. The others shouted and pointed too, urging him to look this way or that. But despite all this, Dudley just stood there, head lowered, silent and still. The poor little ram looked half dead, and nothing the others said or did could rouse him.

Dudley's indifference irritated the other rams. They joked scornfully about "the Dud" and laughed their approval when Lou jostled him roughly and egged him on. But soon their full attention was drawn again to the pit. Apparently something unusual was going on down there, for the rams bantered excitedly among themselves. Crowding closer than ever at the edge, they strained forward for a better view. *I sure hope that's a shallow pit*, thought Sherman. *If anyone slips, he'll fall in for sure!*

But the rams obviously did not share Sherman's concern. They were so bewitched that they noticed no danger at all. Nor did they notice something else: Dudley, taking advantage of their distraction, had quietly pulled back from the rest, slipped away, and returned to the shadow of his rock.

Sherman, who had seen everything, found himself staring sadly at the little black ram. Earlier, Dudley had seemed so content, carefully searching the sky for birds and singing quietly out of a full heart. Now he lay flat against the ground, his head slumped on his legs like a tired dog.

Sherman no longer felt curiosity about the pit. He only wanted one thing: to leave. And—very quietly—that is just what he did.

Reaching the trail, Sherman turned around for a final look at Dudley. The black sheep had not moved. A great sadness filled Sherman's heart. He felt as if he were turning his back on a friend. "But what could I do?" he asked himself. "Besides, maybe they have a good reason for treating him that way." The more he thought about it, the more confused he got. But in the end Sherman did indeed turn his back on Dudley — and he headed out once again for the top of Sin Mountain.

8
THE LONG NIGHT

Lost in thought about his strange experience at the pit, Sherman ambled slowly up the trail. The shadows crept quietly around him. It was only after stumbling a third time that he finally awoke to a shocking truth: the sun had set!

Suddenly, danger lurked everywhere. In the growing darkness he could barely see the path, which had become narrow and treacherous. To his right the canyon cut away so awesomely deep that he dared not even look. And to make matters worse, he was tired and troubled by the events of the day.

Again Sherman considered abandoning his quest. But looking up through the twilight, he could clearly see the clouded mountaintop and the dark silhouettes of the eagles. How could he give up when he had almost reached his goal? "I'm so close!" cried Sherman aloud.

A plan entered his mind. "If I'm going to make it to the top and still get home sometime tonight, there's only one thing left to do." So, aiming himself straight towards the top of the mountain, Sherman did it. Leaping impulsively from the trail, he bounded upwards on the sheer mountain rock.

In less than a second, however, he realized his mistake—for the "sheer mountain rock" was really shale. Before Sherman had taken three jumps, the rock gave way, his hoofs slipped out from beneath him, and he found himself being swept backwards on a carpet of stone, tumbling towards the abyss below.

Sherman bleated at the top of his voice. He scrambled with his legs. He clawed with his hoofs. He tried with all his might to cling to the mountainside, but it was no use: he couldn't stop the fall. Terror filled his heart. Sherman shut his eyes and prepared to die.

Then, something caught him — a tiny ledge, jutting out from the cliff wall. Sherman clung to it desperately, as the rocks and gravel cascaded over his trembling body. Would it hold him? He listened to the rocks clattering into the depths below until, at last, all was silent. Then, after an endless moment, he slowly opened his eyes.

Looking straight ahead, Sherman could see nothing at all — only an ocean of black, empty space. He knew immediately that he was looking out over the vast canyon. His head began to spin, but somehow he managed to lift his eyes. And there, six or seven feet above him, was the trail.

Instantly, Sherman understood his situation. The trail was his only hope. If he could reach it, he could make his way home. If not, he would surely die on this mountain ledge.

Springing to his feet, Sherman reared up on his hind legs and jumped for the trail. He missed. He jumped — and missed again. And again. And again. Over and over he tried, but the trail remained out of reach. Finally, having jumped for nearly an hour, he collapsed in utter defeat.

Night fell and darkness came. Then even the star-light disappeared, swallowed up by a strange fog creeping down the face of the mountain. Sherman lay trembling on the ledge, his mind racing, desperately searching for a way of escape. But it was no use. As the fog engulfed him, Sherman lost all hope, and his father's words replayed in his mind: "Believe me, Son, the only thing you'll discover on the heights of Sin Mountain is trouble. Big trouble. Maybe even death."

Yes, Sherman now realized that this really was Sin Mountain and not "Pleasure Mountain" at all. His father had been right. The little voice in his heart had been right. He had been wrong.

Sherman had fooled himself. He had let himself believe that he was very wise and grown up, imagining that wisdom and maturity simply meant planning fun things and doing them all on your own. But now, hopelessly trapped on this ledge, Sherman was waking up to the truth. He was beginning to understand that even a full-grown ram is no match for the deceitfulness of his own heart—let alone the temptations of Sin Mountain. And with that, he also saw that no matter how old a sheep may be, he will always need someone to lead and care for him. In short, Sherman found that he was still a little lamb, and that in many important ways he always would be.

So Sherman now did what any lamb would do. Alone, afraid, and helpless, he lifted his voice against the night and began to bleat with all his strength, "HELP ME! … HELP ME! … HELP ME!" It was not yet a perfect cry, but it was perfectly sincere—the kind of cry that will always be heard.

And so it went, hour after hour, Sherman bleating out his cry for help; waiting, listening, crying out again. He felt he dare not stop, for time was against him. But finally, after so long a day, exhausted and strained, he ceased. "I'll just rest for a moment or two," said Sherman to himself.

A moment or two later he was fast asleep.

9
A NEW DAY

Whether it was the cold, or the moonlight, or the strange sound echoing in his mind — something woke him. Sherman opened his eyes but didn't move.

"Where am I?" he asked. Then, in a chilling instant, he remembered everything: the mountain, the trees, the berries, the crack, the pit, the fall, the ledge. Everything. But before he had time to think further, he heard the sound again.

"Whooooosh … whooooosh … whooooosh." It was forceful, deliberate, rhythmic. And every time he heard it, almost instantly a gust of wind would brush by his face. Suddenly Sherman realized what it was. It was the sound of wings—huge, powerful wings, cutting through the air above his head.

"HELP ME!" cried Sherman, springing to his feet, "HELP ME! … HELP ME!"

He was afraid to look, but it was impossible not to, for the sight almost filled the nighttime sky. There, wheeling in big circles above him was the largest bird he had ever seen in his life.

The eagles! he thought. But as Sherman looked closer, he saw nothing of the majestic beauty of an eagle. The slick, black plumage, glowing eerily in the moonlight, and the small, gnarled head convinced him of the terrible truth. Sherman gasped, "A vulture!"

Now Sherman cried louder than ever. He knew all too well why the vulture was there—it was waiting for him to die. But Sherman's cries barely fazed the bird: it pulled up slightly, then continued as before—circling, circling, circling, patiently waiting for the end.

The long night was almost over. The eastern horizon was now turning white, and the stars were fading before the coming sun. But Sherman hardly noticed. Tired, cold, and hungry, he only knew that his very life was now flowing from him. He had just enough strength to cry a little and listen much.

"Perhaps …" said Sherman, as if in a dream, "… perhaps the Shepherd will come. He was so good to us. How foolish I was to wander away."

But in his heart Sherman didn't really believe the Shepherd would come. Had he not disobeyed his father? Had he not time and again ignored the little voice speaking in his heart? Had he not stubbornly insisted on his own way? Over and again, his foolish deeds stood up to accuse him. Like thieves breaking in, they beat him down and stole his every hope. "No, the Shepherd will never come," he said in despair. "And who could blame Him after all I've done?"

Yet, when Sherman thought again about the Shepherd's goodness, a tiny blade of hope sprang up in his heart. "But maybe—just maybe—He will come." So, as the sun's rays began pouring over the horizon, Sherman once more gave out a pathetic little cry—and listened.

This time, however, he heard something. A sound came from far above him, from the very top of the mountain. Faintly—but quite clearly—something howled.

"Arrr, arrr, arrrooooooooooo …"

Echoes rolled down the mountain like flood waters trying to swallow up everything in their way. A chill shot straight through Sherman's body and almost stopped his heart. He lay completely motionless, hardly daring to breathe.

"Maybe I just thought I heard it. Maybe it will go away; maybe—"

Then he heard it again, only louder and closer:

"Arrroooooooo."

This time Sherman knew exactly what it was. "A wolf!" he cried. And he was right—but only partly right. This was not just *any* wolf, but *the* wolf, the father of all the wolves in this territory. And just as Bertram had said, it was an enemy the likes of which Sherman had never seen nor even imagined.

Now, at this point Sherman did something that you might think was very foolish. But when sheep are in a panic, they yield to all kinds of foolishness. So Sherman leaped to his feet. His legs were shaking so violently he could barely stand. He cried out wildly, "HELP ME! HELP ME! HELP ME!"

This, of course, was exactly the wrong thing to do, for each cry only guided the wolf and brought it closer. But poor Sherman was completely confused. The wolf would howl, Sherman would cry, and the wolf would draw closer still.

Then the howling stopped. Frozen stiff, Sherman listened with all his might. He now could hear the sound of heavy steps making their way towards him on the rocks above. Seconds later he heard breathing. Then, when the breathing became quite loud, the footsteps ceased. Sherman could hear nothing but heavy panting directly overhead — and the wild beating of his own heart.

Sherman stood as if paralyzed. An evil presence pressed him on every side. He could neither speak nor move. He did, however, manage to lift his eyes, not because he wanted to, but because everything — even the light of dawn itself — seemed drawn into the dark presence above him. Suddenly, Sherman was staring directly into the face of the wolf.

A huge head hung in the air above him. Motionless and silent, its grey eyes darted back and forth, scanning him from head to foot. Then they too stopped. The wolf simply stared eye-to-eye at its helpless prey.

Slowly its mouth began to move. For a split second the twisted lips seemed actually to be smiling, as if this moment brought the wolf some strange delight. But then its face changed. Its eyes filled with hatred, and its gleaming teeth were bared. From the depths of its huge grey body, there arose a low, angry growl. "One of His own," hissed the wolf with contempt. And then it lunged forward, hungrily jutting its enormous neck down the rock wall towards Sherman.

With one great sweep of his eyes Sherman looked first at the canyon below, then at the vulture circling above, and finally at the wolf's head stretching down at him. There was nowhere — absolutely nowhere — to turn.

And then something very painful, but very important happened: Sherman's heart melted within him. In fact, so thoroughly did it melt, you might even say he died. For in that terrible moment the old Sherman — the clever, confident, foolish young ram — completely dissolved like snow in warm water. His legs collapsed beneath him. His body curled itself into a little ball. He closed his eyes. And then, barely whispering, Sherman the sheep cried out perfectly for the first time in his whole life. "God, I'm so sorry; please, please help me." And he wept like a baby lamb.

Now when a sheep is broken and crying like a baby lamb, he isn't much aware of what's going on around him. So it took a while for Sherman to notice something strange. Yes, the wolf was still growling, but now the sound seemed fainter.

Full of fear, Sherman opened one eye and glanced up. A ray of hope entered his heart: the wolf was out of sight!

But just as quickly, Sherman realized that the wolf was not leaving. No, something—or someone— was now up there with him, and the wolf was growling at *it*! The sound sent chills along his back.

It made him think of sheep dogs facing off to fight. Sherman could imagine the wolf frozen in place, muscles tensed, ears flattened back, eyes glaring, and teeth bared to the gums. It was ready to spring against its adversary … whoever that was.

Suddenly, the low, steady growl exploded into a frenzy of snarling, and there was a great commotion on the rocks above. Dust whirled in the air. Rocks rolled down the mountain. Barking and growling echoed through the canyon. The wolf had attacked.

Sherman heard a dull thud, like the sound of a club hitting a saddlebag. The wolf wailed. Fury filled its voice.

But it attacked again.

Then came a grunt, another sickening thud, and more wailing, worse than before. Yet the wolf attacked again— and again and again. It was taking a terrible beating, but its hatred brought it back for more and more.

Finally, the wolf received such a mighty blow that Sherman could actually hear it rolling over the rocks. And this time it wailed, not in fury, but in pain. An agonized yelp echoed through the canyon. There was more scrambling on the rocks, and more howling, but now from a distance. Could it be that the wolf was fleeing?

Sherman stood breathlessly on his ledge, head down, ears opened, listening intently. Yes, the cries were growing fainter and fainter. The wolf was running away!

Then, when Sherman could barely hear the wolf's cries, something further happened to encourage him. A shadow passed swiftly across his ledge. Sherman looked up. For a moment, the sun blinded his eyes. But then he saw it: the vulture was fleeing, too! Sherman watched as the great black form gradually faded from sight, disappearing into the clouds above.

The wolf was gone. The vulture was gone. The fight was over. Silence covered the mountain.

Sherman crouched on his ledge, his little body shaking from the ordeal. But now, deep in his heart, he knew everything would be all right. In fact, he felt at peace, almost as if he were lying on the valley floor beside his father and mother.

He noticed a change in his surroundings. The sun, now fully risen, was bright and friendly, and the air warm and playful. The tired old mountain itself seemed to stir, as if some ancient beauty, locked beneath its scarred surface, was struggling to rise in honor of an important guest.

Where have I felt this peace before? wondered Sherman. And then he remembered. He had felt it around the evening campfires, when the Good Shepherd would play his harp and sing for the flock. He thought of his father and mother and all his relatives, gathered in a big circle under the starry sky. He thought of the little lambs who always sat beside him and looked up to him. And he thought of the Shepherd, seated on a rock, His rod and staff close at hand, playing on the harp and singing the songs of God. Those beautiful, beautiful melodies … why, he could almost hear them now!

Suddenly, Sherman was overcome. He lay down on his ledge, buried his dusty face in his legs, and wept. For in that moment Sherman realized how good the Shepherd really was, and how much He loved him.

Then something very interesting happened. As Sherman lay there weeping and thinking about the Shepherd's love, he felt a hand on the back of his neck! Now the interesting thing is that he wasn't even scared, for deep in his heart he already knew who it was (and I bet you know, too!). For a brief instant, Sherman hung in the air like a kitten in its mother's mouth—and the next thing he knew, he was safe in the Shepherd's arms.

Well, if you've ever had a puppy greet you, then you know a little bit how Sherman greeted his Master. He was no big tough ram that day! He licked the Shepherd's face, wiggled and twisted in His arms, nuzzled against His chest, and bleated and baahhed at the top of his lungs.

As for the Shepherd—He laughed and laughed, tears of joy rolling down His face. "Yes, yes, little friend, it's good to be together again."

To Sherman those words were sweeter than honey. After all he'd done, the Shepherd still called him His "little friend." In days to come, when Sherman was back with the flock, he would often ponder those special words, realizing that there was nothing he could ever do to deserve so great a friendship. But he would also determine with all his might never to abuse that friendship again.

For now, though, Sherman was too excited to think much at all. The Shepherd knelt down, searching Sherman's body for wounds, and giving him a drink from His waterskin. Sherman felt so happy that he hardly noticed how tired the Shepherd looked, or how His robe was torn and matted with dust. He only knew that he was safe in the Shepherd's care. And that was where he planned to stay!

"Well, Sherman," said the Shepherd, "we'd better get going. You have some worried friends waiting down below."

These words saddened Sherman. They made him yearn to rejoin his loved ones and to put their hearts at rest. As if He understood, the Shepherd picked up His eager companion and cradled him in His right arm. While Sherman nestled against Him, the Shepherd glanced upwards at the mountaintop. For an instant, His features strained and His eyes filled with pity. Then, as quickly as it came, the look was gone. The Shepherd straightened Himself, turned, pressed Sherman close to His side, and headed briskly down the mountain.

10
HOMEWARD BOUND

The Shepherd Himself seemed eager to get home. He walked with long, powerful strides, always looking straight ahead, never stopping to rest.

Sherman, secure in the Shepherd's embrace, looked all around and could hardly believe what he was seeing. Earlier, when he was alone, the mountain had seemed so mysterious and inviting. Now, viewed from the Shepherd's arms, he saw how barren and ugly it really was.

"Why, this place is stupid!" said Sherman angrily.

But when he thought about how easily it had deceived him—and how it nearly took his life—Sherman's anger gave way to fear. He nestled deeper in the crook of the Shepherd's arm.

As they descended the mountain, Sherman realized they were approaching the pit where he had spied on the other sheep. His heart stirred with expectancy. Was the little black ram still beneath his rock? Was he all right?

Then, rounding a bend in the trail, Sherman caught a clear view of the pit and the rock nearby. There was no sheep there. His heart sank. *Well*, he thought, trying to keep up his hopes, *maybe I'll see him farther down the trail*. But remembering the cruelty of the other rams—especially the big one—Sherman secretly feared he would never see the little black ram again.

The Shepherd marched on vigorously, making excellent time. Still, it was hard for Sherman to wait. He was eager to see his family, but for some reason he was even more eager to see that little ram. Sherman even found himself praying for Dudley, and wishing that somehow the Shepherd might take him for His own.

What am I thinking? said Sherman to himself, shocked at the content of his own prayer. *That little sheep belongs to someone else, and the Shepherd would never steal!* But the yearning to see Dudley in the Shepherd's flock simply wouldn't leave him. So Sherman prayed on, putting the matter in God's hands and asking Him to find a way.

The morning sun was now almost directly overhead and Sherman recognized the terrain. Soon they would pass the tree with the great crack around it.

The thought of it made him shiver. But just then something happened that made him forget his fears: he heard sounds—sheep sounds! Sherman's heart raced. Could it be them? Could it be him? And as the Shepherd (who Himself seemed to walk more quickly) again turned the bend, Sherman saw that indeed it was.

There, all too near the crack, huddled the gang of rams (who seemed fewer than before), wrapped in a thick cloud of yellow smoke billowing up from under the depths of the earth. A few lay on the ground, almost unconscious, murmuring to themselves. But most staggered to and fro on their feet, laughing wildly in the midst of the cloud. Nickey was there, and his bodyguard, Lou. The other rams seemed to follow those two around—though in fact, they all were following the cloud of smoke, which slowly drew them nearer and nearer to the edge of the crack.

Sherman looked around, trying urgently to find the black sheep. "There he is!" cried Sherman, leaping in the Shepherd's arms. Yes, there, on the far side of the clearing, beyond the reach of the smoke, stood the little black ram. All alone—with bewilderment in his face—he watched his friends.

Then Sherman heard a loud, high-pitched whistle. It didn't exactly scare him (because he knew that sound well), but it did make him jump—for it came from right above his head. Immediately, he realized what was happening. And then he jumped again—this time for joy. It was the Shepherd whistling. This was the way He always called His sheep.

The other rams must have heard the sound, for a few of them lifted their heads and glanced towards the Shepherd. But seconds later they turned again to their play in the smoke.

With Dudley, however, things were very different. When he heard the whistle, all four feet left the ground. He sprang into the air as though a lion's roar had startled him out of his sleep! Quickly, he turned to look, and in an instant his eyes were riveted on the Good Shepherd.

As the two gazed at one another, Sherman studied their faces—and what he saw in that moment he would remember for a lifetime. The Shepherd's eyes were filled with compassion and longing. Sherman had seen such a look only a few times in his life, usually on the face of his father when one of the lambs was sick or injured. But there was also a solemnity on the Shepherd's face. Sherman could tell that He would not whistle again. Rather, as if in obedience to some unknown law, He would now wait for the little ram to respond.

Would he come or would he hold back? Would he ever get another chance to come? Sherman sensed that for the little black ram this was a crucial moment—perhaps the most important of his whole life. And looking at the Shepherd's face, he saw that his Master sensed it too.

As for Dudley, he seemed surprised—even alarmed. And for good reason. He had never dreamed of facing such a decision. An unknown Shepherd was calling him to leave both his flock and his whole way of life to follow Him. Yes, that life was mostly empty, and often painful—but it was the only life he had ever known. How could he simply abandon it to follow a total stranger? What would the other rams do if they saw him leave? And worst of all, what if his own shepherds found out, got angry, and came after him? Like weeds, the questions wrapped themselves around him, gripping him with fear.

But as Dudley thought again of the clear, strong whistle, and as he searched the stranger's face, he felt his heart grow calm. No, he concluded, there was no real danger—not from this man, anyway. In fact, looking into the Shepherd's eyes, Dudley began to experience something he had never known before. He didn't even have a word for it (though Sherman would easily have recognized it as *hope*). He only knew that somehow, at least for a moment, he could see into the future—and the future was bright with goodness and joy. So Dudley said "yes" to that future—and began walking slowly towards the Good Shepherd.

Sherman watched and saw an amazing transformation. It seemed that Dudley's every step brought him more powerfully under the healing influence of the Shepherd's love. His pace grew bold. His head was lifted high. His eyes glistened bright. He was a completely different ram!

Watching Dudley, Sherman thought of dawn in those high mountain valleys known only to the Shepherd. The warm, golden sunlight would slowly push back the shadows to reveal a glistening, dew-drenched meadow, bursting with life and color. Such mornings had often awed Sherman with their beauty, and filled him with a joy that brought tears to his eyes. And yet, for all their beauty, those dawns could not compare with what he now saw on the face of Dudley, the little black sheep.

"Hey, Dud, where ya goin'?" The voice was

pleasant and smooth as butter — but it instantly shattered the atmosphere of joy. Sherman turned and saw two big rams making their way towards the black sheep. Then he turned again and looked at Dudley. The newfound strength was pouring out of his body like water onto the ground. Soon it was the old Dudley once again, eyes downcast, cowering guiltily before the oncoming rams. Sherman's heart began to pound: he feared for the little black ram.

"Say nothing at all, Sherman." The words of the Shepherd were gentle, but very firm. Sherman knew it was important to obey.

"So who're your new friends, Dudley? Why don't you introduce us?" It was Nickey who called out the questions. He and Lou had stopped at a safe distance, eyeing the Shepherd from twenty yards away. Dudley, who was much closer to the Shepherd, stood alone and still, as if paralyzed between the two opposing influences.

"I … I don't know, Nickey. I was just about to introduce myself and find out."

"Well, I guess you'd better save it for next time. It's gettin' late and we gotta be gettin' down the mountain." Nickey turned around, motioned with his shoulder, and issued a sharp command. "Come on, Dud, let's go."

Dudley stared guiltily at the ground, scraping the dirt beneath his hoofs. But he took no step.

"Hey, Dud, I said it's getting late." Now Nickey sounded angry. "Quit messin' around and come on."

"You guys go ahead. I want to meet these folks. I'll see you later." Dudley's voice trembled, but even so, they made Sherman's heart leap with joy.

Nickey turned around again. He had a serious look on his face. He took several risky steps towards the little ram, then he stood for a few seconds in silence, as if considering his strategy. Finally, he spoke—and his words poured forth like venom from a snake.

"Okay, Dudley, let's get real." At those words, Dudley visibly cringed. Nickey continued, "We all heard this guy whistle, and we all know what that means. So you can leave the flock if you want— that's the law of the land, and I can't stop you." He paused, as if daring Dudley to go.

"And ya know, right about now, I'm not so sure I want you to stay." Nickey sounded hurt, as if he'd been betrayed. "Ya know, Dud, you've got a few enemies around here. But in case you haven't noticed, I've been standin' up for you all along, tryin' to help you break in with the guys. In fact, it could be I'm the best friend you've got—not that it does me any good!"

Dudley lowered his eyes in shame.

"Anyway, Dud, whether you wanna be friends or not—that's up to you. But I've still got my job to do. The shepherds put me in charge of you guys, to show you a good time and get you back to the flock safe and sound. Now maybe you don't figure I've been showin' you a good time—but I'm still not gonna let you get killed without a fight."

Lou gazed at Nickey with admiration. Dudley stood motionless, frozen with fear.

Sherman, observing the deadly influence of Nickey's words on Dudley, felt sick at heart. *Why doesn't the Shepherd do something?*

But Nickey continued, "I mean, what do you

know about this guy, anyway? Do you know how he's gonna treat you? Who's to say he won't serve you up for supper tonight?" Nickey paused, giving Dudley plenty of time to imagine such a fate. And apparently that is just what Dudley did: once again his legs were melting and his body swaying, exactly as they had done the day before.

"An' I'll tell ya somethin' else, Dud. I've seen his flock around these parts before. Smallest flock I've ever seen. Ever ask yourself why? How come he can't get any sheep to follow him? And the ones that do—well, the truth is, Dud, they're losers, weaklings that just can't make it on their own. That's not what you want, Dud—not if you want to be a real ram."

Nickey fell silent again. The air was tense. It was clear that in a moment Dudley would have to decide.

"One last thing, Dud. Now I don't wanna scare ya, but … well, I'm not so sure how our shepherds would take it if you left. Yeah, I know it's the law of the land—you can choose who you wanna follow. But when those shepherds get riled up … well, they don't much care about the law." Nickey glanced at the Shepherd and Sherman. "Things could get pretty ugly for these guys." He paused. "And for you, too."

Hearing these words, Dudley finally slipped to the ground. Nickey and Lou glanced at one another, looking deeply satisfied.

The two rams turned around as if to leave. With a note of concern in his voice, Nickey offered a parting remark. "Don't get me wrong, Dud. If the shepherds get you back, I'd still want to be your friend. But how could I keep on protecting you, once you'd turned your back on all the guys? It just wouldn't be fair to them. No, Dud, I'm afraid you'd just have to make it on your own." Nickey paused to let the words sink in. Then, resignedly, he concluded. "Well, Dud, I've said all I can. Now it's up to you. But if you're smart, you'll come with us."

With Lou behind him, Nickey walked away towards the crack. Dudley lifted his head. He looked terrified, as if he were being left to die in the wilderness. Seeing it, Sherman pleaded in his heart with the little ram. *Don't listen to him, don't listen to his lies!* But Dudley had listened — not just to Nickey's lies, but to his own fears. The joy he had shown only moments earlier as he approached the Shepherd, was gone. Now, in its place, there was nothing but horror at Nickey's terrible parting words, "… you'll just have to make it on your own."

The thought was evidently more than Dudley

could bear. "Wait!" he cried at the top of his voice, "… wait for me!" And with that, he leaped up and ran with all his might to rejoin his old familiar friends.

Now at this point—even though he didn't mean to—Sherman disobeyed the Shepherd. At the top of his voice he cried out to Dudley, "Don't do it! Don't go. … Come back!" But Dudley never even turned his head.

Then Sherman squirmed frantically, hoping to slip from the Shepherd's arms and chase after Dudley. But the Shepherd, holding him tighter than ever, quickly turned His back on the young rams, and headed for the trail.

"That's my friend!" cried Sherman. "… Please, please let me go get my friend!" He struggled violently to free himself, but the Shepherd held him all the more firmly in His grip. He squirmed and squirmed, but to no avail. Finally, as the whole terrible scene faded from sight, Sherman surrendered and slumped in despair against His master's breast.

"Oh, what will they do to Dudley?" he cried, as the Shepherd carried him farther and farther from his friend. "Will they make him smell the smoke? What if he falls in the crack?" The questions, the imaginings, the terrible possibilities raged like a storm within him. But that was not the worst of it. Sherman was not only afraid for Dudley — he was confused and disappointed in the Shepherd.

Why didn't He do something? Surely He could have scared off those rams. Why did He just stand there? The more questions he asked, the harder he found it not to be angry with his Master.

For over an hour they traveled along in silence.

Feeling betrayed, Sherman withdrew from the Shepherd's touch. Like a deadly night-time fog, bitter anger crept into his heart.

Then, something unexpected happened: rounding a sharp curve on the lower slopes of the mountain, the Shepherd left the trail. He stopped on a little promontory overlooking the valley below.

As Sherman looked down, he immediately noticed a huge flock of sheep camped at the foot of the mountain. It was the flock of his former friends. Then, after much searching, he finally saw in the distance what he was looking for — the Shepherd's little flock, grazing in a lonely meadow to the west. A spring of joy erupted in his heart, swirling around the anger, threatening to wash it away. Just then the Shepherd spoke.

"You are wondering why I didn't help your little

friend," He said in a voice that carried no accusation.

The Shepherd knew all about his anger! Sherman was amazed … and embarrassed, too. But the more he thought about it, the more he found himself comforted. Yes, somehow the Shepherd knew what was in his heart—but in spite of that, He hadn't put him down or scolded him at all. Not only did the Shepherd know; He also understood.

"Sherman, look at that flock beneath us." The Shepherd pointed to the huge flock milling about at the base of the mountain.

"Every sheep you see there is exactly where he wants to be. Some are perfectly content, others dream of change. But in the end they're all where they choose to be. This is the law of the land, Sherman, and I cannot change it." The Shepherd paused, letting the words sink deep into Sherman's heart.

"Now look at our little flock, there in the far meadow." Sherman lifted his eyes and looked until he spotted them again—a few pin-pricks of bright white on a carpet of green.

"I called each one of them," said the Shepherd. "And many came from the flocks of the worthless shepherds who camp at the foot of this mountain. All of those sheep were afraid, too. Nevertheless, they chose to follow Me. ... Your little friend did not."

The words were hard to bear, but Sherman could not deny that they were true.

The Shepherd held Sherman a little closer, gently stroking his neck. Suddenly, He chuckled. Sherman felt the rippling laughter flow from the Master's body into his own.

"Back at that tree you heard me whistle. But

your new friend heard something else. He heard Me call his name." The Shepherd paused again, smiling. "Yes, I've had My eyes on little Dudley for quite some time."

Again, Sherman was seized with amazement. The Shepherd already knew Dudley! But *why* did He have His eyes on him?

"He heard it," said the Shepherd thoughtfully, "but with this one there are many, many fears. So perhaps he has not yet heard it completely. Let's not give up, Sherman, but let's give God time. Give God time—and pray."

There was much in the Shepherd's words that Sherman could not understand. But one thing he now knew—there was still hope. Sherman glanced at the little flock in the distant meadow, imagining himself and Dudley grazing together peacefully under the Master's watchful care. Quickly he closed his eyes, nestled close to the Shepherd, and fervently prayed.

When he opened his eyes a few moments later, his heart was at peace. He was ready to go home.

11
A ROUGH REUNION

Sherman wanted very much to rejoin his loved ones. But, as you can well imagine, he was hardly eager to face his father. How could he explain where he'd been and what he'd done? Thinking about it made him feel a little sick. If only he could make himself invisible!

But when at last they approached the camp and Sherman saw his faithful friends posted right where the Shepherd had left them, heads bobbing with excitement and joy, well … that was the end of his fears! And when he saw his mother, Eunice, standing at the front of the flock, he squirmed and wiggled so wildly that the Shepherd had to put him down. In an instant he was with them all.

Now, as you probably know, sheep don't hug — they rub. So there they were, the whole flock trying to get beside Sherman to greet him with a loving rub. Of course they didn't all succeed, for in the cloud of dust they raised, they could barely see one another. But eventually everybody rubbed somebody else, and much, much joy was passed among the flock that day.

As things calmed down and the sheep began to disperse, Sherman realized that all the family was there except his father. Nervously he looked around. It wasn't long before he saw Bertram standing alone under a distant olive tree, the place they had often gone when they needed to discuss his behavior.

Sherman didn't like the looks of this, but he

loved his father very much. And how could they be together again, following the Shepherd with joy, if he didn't confess to his dad what he had done? It was going to be hard, but Sherman decided he'd better just do it and get it over with. There would never be a better or easier time.

It was a long walk to the olive tree, even with his mother Eunice at his side. The situation seemed unbearably grim. *Perhaps*, thought Sherman, *I could lighten things up*. So he tried wiggling his tail very fast, like the little lambs. This looked cute, and had sometimes helped him during past discussions. But it was no use. The closer he got to his father, the more he felt the seriousness of all he had done, so that by the time he reached the tree his tail was flat against his bottom in shame. Sherman stood completely still, staring at the ground. He couldn't even lift up his eyes to look his father in the face.

Bertram drew close to Sherman's side. "We're glad you're home, Son. Your mother and I … well, I guess you'd say we were pretty worried. But the Shepherd has brought you back. You're home safe, and we're grateful."

Sherman tried, but he could not receive the comfort. "I've brought shame on you and Mother and our whole family," he replied, wishing his father could say something to undo the damage, yet feeling sure he couldn't.

"The lambs don't know where you went, Sherman."

For a moment, Sherman felt relieved. Then sadness clouded his face again. "But you know, and Mother knows—and your friends know. I've hurt and disappointed you, and there's nothing I can do.

I'm sorry Father, I really am." Sherman was now looking into his father's face, his eyes brimming with tears.

"You've done the important thing, Son. You've said you're sorry, and you've come home. We forgive you."

The words were precious to Sherman. Like a medicine, they began to heal the ache in his heart.

The three of them stood together silently for a long moment. Then, quite suddenly, Sherman perked up his head and announced, "All right, Father, I'm ready for my spanking now."

Bertram looked surprised. He pondered for a moment, while gazing proudly at his disheveled son. Then he said, "How about if we forget the spanking, Sherman? Looking at you, I'd say you've learned your lesson well enough."

"No, Father, you told me not to go up Sin Mountain, and I did. Besides, all the lambs are watching, and I want them to see. Maybe it will help them obey their mothers and fathers."

Bertram glanced across the field. Sure enough, the lambs were all huddled together. And every one of them had that "look" that says they're not looking, when really they are. So Bertram reluctantly agreed.

"All right, Son, if you insist." And Bertram stood on his hind legs, bit off a branch from the tree, laid it on the ground, and began nibbling at the leaves.

Now while Bertram was preparing the switch, Eunice had been watching Sherman. Suddenly she let out a piercing bleat.

"Sherman!" she cried, "you're hurt!"

Bertram leaped up and ran to her side.

"Look!" she said. And as Bertram looked, his heart froze. Sherman's rump, which he had bravely presented for the spanking, was covered with blood.

"Sherman, are you all right?" cried Bertram. And before he could answer, both parents were nosing through Sherman's wool, trying to find the wound.

"I feel fine, Father. What's wrong? What do you see?" asked Sherman.

"There's blood on your back," said Bertram quietly, trying to conceal his anxiety. "Did you fall or cut yourself?"

"Well, I did take a fall, but I don't think I cut myself."

The worried parents kept searching anyway — searching and searching for the source of the blood.

"Really, Father, I'm fine," said Sherman impatiently.

"Well, this blood had to come from somewhere, Son," answered Bertram, with growing frustration in his voice.

Now when his father said that, a terrible thought flashed into Sherman's mind. He grew very still and very silent. Then, after a few moments, he spoke in a low, trembling voice. "You don't have to look any-more, Father. I know where the blood came from." There was deep sorrow in every word.

"Well, tell us then," said Bertram.

Sherman whispered, "It's the Shepherd's blood."

"The Shepherd's blood!" gasped Eunice. "What do you mean?"

Sherman told the story as briefly as he could. "When I was up on the mountain, I fell onto a ledge and I was there all night. At dawn a wolf came. He leaned over the ledge to get me, but just then the

Shepherd arrived. There was a horrible fight, but the wolf finally ran away. Then the Shepherd reached down and picked me up and held me in His arms. All the way down the mountain He held me close to His side. It came from His side, Mother. The blood came from the Shepherd's side."

The three of them stood silently looking at each other. Bertram knew it was true. So did Eunice. They felt sorry for their son, but there was nothing they could say.

"Could I go now, Dad?" asked Sherman quietly.

His father nodded. "Go ahead, Sherman. We can talk later."

So Sherman turned and slowly walked away.

Well, if you know anything about parents, you know it was a long, difficult day for Bertram and Eunice. Their son had been through so much, and they greatly desired to comfort him. But for now they felt it best to leave him alone. They decided simply to go about their business, hoping to see him that night at the campfire.

Sure enough, they did. Just as the Shepherd began to tune his harp, Sherman appeared out of nowhere and sat down. As usual, the little lambs gathered at his feet and looked up at him. In fact, everyone was staring at him. They didn't want to, but they couldn't help it. Yes, they were glad to have him back. But it was more than that. Something about Sherman had changed. His parents noticed it right away. And they also noticed—much to their amazement—that the blood was gone. Sherman's coat was bright and clean.

The Shepherd leaned His harp against a rock, stood and began to speak.

"Well, little friends, we have much to be grateful for tonight. God has blessed us all, and Sherman is home safe and sound." A murmur of approval rippled through the flock. Then, looking thoughtful, the Shepherd spoke again.

"Have I told you before how dangerous these parts are?" He asked. "Yes, I'm sure I have. But listen—all of you—once again.

"The land you see around us belongs to My Father. And yet this land is not our home, for long ago it fell into the hands of an enemy. Someday I will take it back for My Father. But until then I must gather My flock, care for it, and protect it from our enemy. Do you remember My telling you these things?" All the sheep nodded that they did.

"Then remember this too. Whatever is good—truly good—in due time I will lead you to it.

But whatever is not good … well, you may be sure that I will pass it by—for like our enemy, it can only hurt and destroy. I know this land very well. I know what is good, and I know what is not. That is why you must all follow Me. You have nothing to fear, if only you will follow Me. Do you understand?"

Again the sheep nodded their heads—and fastened their eyes on the Shepherd. They knew their Master well. They could see from His smile that He was feeling merry. The Good Shepherd was about to celebrate!

"And now," said the Shepherd, as the flock glanced knowingly at each other, "let us rejoice together, for I have found my sheep who was lost."

With these words, the Shepherd lifted His harp and began to play one of His favorite tunes. The sparkling melody poured over the flock like a mountain stream. Tails began to twitter, hoofs began to tap, whole bodies began to bounce up and down. Yes, everyone felt the call of the dance!

Now anyone who has seen sheep has probably seen them dancing, though most folks wouldn't think to use that word. To us humans, a sheep dance looks more like a frolic—a bright medley of completely unexpected motions, including spurts, spins, twitches, switches, kicks, stops, hops, starts, leaps, bleats and *baahhs*. Well, that's exactly what the Shepherd's flock began to do. In the way they knew best—in the language of the dance—they all expressed their joy and gratitude, praising God that Sherman was home at last, and that they, like him, had somehow found a place in the flock of the Good Shepherd.

How long it went on, I cannot tell. But when at

last the Shepherd concluded His song with a great crescendo of melody, the flock all fell to the ground, leaving dizzy heaps of sheep scattered everywhere, laughing and singing for joy.

Yes, you should have seen them. But more than that, you should have seen the Shepherd. Never again would you doubt (if ever you did) that the Shepherd loves His flock—and that He loves playing with them, too! As a matter of fact, some of us who have seen His enthusiasm for play, secretly think He invented it Himself!

But alas, on this night playing was the farthest thing from Sherman's troubled mind. Watching the flock from his place on the sidelines, he could only see the ways in which his trip up Sin Mountain had hurt each one of them. Was there nothing he could do to make it right? Could he ever again look them in the eyes and rejoice among them as they were rejoicing tonight?

His heart was indeed heavy. But as the dancing reached its climax, an idea took shape in Sherman's mind. Yes, there was something he could do. It didn't seem like much, but it was better than nothing at all. Sherman began waiting for the right moment … and praying for the courage to do what he had to do.

The evening was drawing to a close. The Shepherd, smiling and breathless, assembled the flock at His feet. He told them how much He had enjoyed the evening. He told them to get a good rest, for soon they must return to His Father's house. Then He asked them to bow their heads while He sang to them the evening prayer.

The prayer bound all together in a gentle peace,

and as it concluded, the sheep lingered in silence, each one lost in his own thoughts. Sherman knew his moment had come. He slowly rose and stepped forward into their midst. Unsurprised, the sheep lifted their eyes and waited for him to speak. Sherman stared at the ground, groping for words.

"I know it's late, and I'll only take a moment. But there's something I'd like to say."

Sherman looked at the lambs. "Maybe this is especially for you lambs. I hope it will help you not to … well, I just hope it will help you." The lambs began to fidget.

"Earlier tonight the Shepherd said He would never lead us in a way that wasn't good, for those are ways that hurt and destroy. Well, what I have learned today is that when we choose those ways, it's not just ourselves we hurt. We hurt others too."

Sherman paused, then looked into his parent's eyes. "We hurt our mother and father, disappoint them, and make them worry."

He paused again, gazing at the rest of his family and all the lambs. "We set a bad example for our little brothers and sisters, and for those who look up to us."

Sherman paused. Then he lifted his eyes until they met the Shepherd's. "And we can hurt our friends, too ... sometimes very badly."

At this his voice broke, and for the next few moments he wept quietly. Everyone was silent. The little lambs squirmed uncomfortably, but many of the older ones understood. Some even wept with him.

"Anyway," said Sherman, finding new strength, "I just wanted to tell you I'm sorry for the trouble

I caused all of you when I disappeared yesterday. I want to ask you to forgive me."

No one moved and no one spoke. Sherman had no idea what would happen next. But one thing he did know. Inside his heart, a little spring of joy had begun to bubble upwards. The burden was gone.

"You're forgiven, little friend," came a voice from behind him. Then Sherman felt the Shepherd's hand stroking his neck affectionately.

When he looked up, Sherman saw the whole flock hurrying towards him. Gathering round, they each gave him a rub and a nuzzle, thanked him for his words, and told him how much they loved him. One by one they kept coming, and as they did, Sherman thought to himself, *The Shepherd was right. These are my friends, the friends God has given me.* Sherman felt they would be his friends forever. They were enough, and more than enough.

"Well," said the Shepherd in a big voice for all to hear, "let's get some rest. Tomorrow we begin our journey back to the lowlands, and to My Father's house."

The flock slowly dispersed in little groups of two and three. Some whispered, some quietly sang, some walked in silence, looking at the stars. But all were savoring the wonder of that special night as they went in peace, each to his or her own place.

As for Bertram and Eunice, their hearts were so full, they couldn't sleep. So they took a stroll beneath the stars and talked. Yes, they agreed, it had been a difficult day for both of them, but deep in their hearts there was peace and joy. Sherman had come home.

12
THE CALL

When Sherman's parents finally returned to the camp, Bertram made his nightly rounds, checking on each of his children. As a rule this was quite a job, with backs to rub, stories to tell, and prayers to lead. But tonight, after the excitement of the day, he found them all fast asleep.

All, that is, except Sherman. He was lying slightly apart from the others, quietly gazing across the grass towards the flickering fire where the Shepherd slept. Bertram sat down beside him. For a long time they sat silently looking towards the Good Shepherd.

"Father," said Sherman, breaking the silence, "why am I here?"

"What do you mean, Son?" asked Bertram.

"What I mean is, why am I here, safe in the Shepherd's care? I've been thinking about what I did. I mean, I knew better, but I went up the mountain anyway. And I went up farther than all the rest! So it seems to me I should be dead! But instead, here I am, safe with the Shepherd, while the others …" (Sherman paused as his thoughts transported him into the dark distance.) "… the others are still up there. I can't understand it, Father."

Bertram grew pensive. Then, after a long moment, he answered. "I'm not sure I understand it either, Son. What I do understand is that for some reason we all belong to the Good Shepherd, and that He takes His charge very seriously." Bertram paused, as a gentle smile spread across his face.

"Once I heard Him say something interesting to those worthless shepherds over by the mountain. There was a disagreement over one of us, and He said, 'My Father has given them to me, and they will never perish. No one will snatch them out of my hand.' You should have heard how He said 'no one'! Needless to say, He got His sheep back!"

Bertram laughed, then looked at his son. "Yes, Sherman, He loves us very much, and no one will ever take us from Him. I don't understand it all, but I understand it enough to be very, very grateful."

The words did not explain everything, but they somehow satisfied Sherman. So the two sheep fell silent, enjoying the delicate beauty of the Shepherd's fire and reflecting on all the things they had learned.

After a while, Sherman again broke the silence.

"Father, can *anyone* belong to the Shepherd's flock?"

Bertram looked at his son. "Anyone who wants to. That's the law of the land here, as you well know."

"Yes, but doesn't the Shepherd have to call you first?"

"Yes, that's true. Why do you ask?"

"Well, what if a sheep says 'yes,' but changes his mind?" asked Sherman, with a troubled look on his face.

"Then I'd say he didn't say 'yes' at all … unless … unless he was confused, or maybe scared, like your Uncle Billy was." (Uncle Billy was not really Sherman's uncle, but Bertram's closest friend. Sherman could not remember a time when Uncle Billy hadn't been around. He was just part of the family — all the more so, now that his wife had passed away.)

Sherman quickly glanced at his father. "What do you mean: 'like Uncle Billy was'?"

Bertram was silent, considering whether or not to answer Sherman's question. Finally, he replied, "Well, I hadn't planned to tell you about that yet."

"Tell me about what?" asked Sherman.

Bertram said nothing. Sherman sprang to his feet. He urged his father to tell him the story.

"Sherman, why are you so excited? What's going on?"

"I'll explain, Father, I promise. But first, tell me about Uncle Billy."

Bertram was puzzled, and even a little suspicious: what had happened up on the mountain to make Sherman so interested in the story about Billy? He lay there thoughtfully searching his son's face for clues.

"Father, please …," cried Sherman, in a voice that echoed over the camp.

"All right, all right," whispered Bertram. "But lie down and be still, or you'll wake up the whole flock." Reluctantly, Sherman obeyed.

Bertram drew a deep breath. "Sherman, your Uncle Billy was not born into the Shepherd's flock." Bertram waited a few seconds, letting the words sink in. "He came to us from another flock, when I was just a young ram like you."

Sherman neither moved nor spoke.

"You're not surprised?" asked Bertram.

"No, I guess I'm not, Father. So much has been happening lately."

Gradually a sense of awe and amazement was settling upon Sherman. Something great was happening, something far bigger than himself. No, he wasn't surprised to learn about Uncle Billy. But he was afraid. He knew that he must not fail to understand all that his father was about to say.

"Now please, Father, tell me the rest of the story."

Even more puzzled by his son's urgency, Bertram continued:

"Well, many years ago some worthless shepherds—just like the ones now camping beneath that mountain—abandoned your Uncle Billy out in the wilderness. He'd gotten sick, and instead of tending to him, they just left him behind to die."

Bertram's voice trembled with anger. But as he paused, lost in thought, a smile spread across his face. "Still, it really is a wonderful story." He spoke the words almost reverently, then a new resolve entered his voice. "You know, Sherman, I probably should have told you about this sooner."

"Father ..." scolded Sherman, coaxing him on.

"All right, all right. Well, one evening the Shepherd and I were walking together, keeping watch while the others grazed. We had stopped to look at the sunset glowing on a nearby mountain. That's when we heard the sound. It was faint, but unmistakable. Somewhere on that mountain a sheep was in trouble.

"Well, you know the Shepherd. Instantly, He started running. And by the time I arrived, He'd sized up the situation perfectly.

"'Up there,' He said, 'in that cave.' I looked where He was pointing, and then I heard another cry. Yes, the Shepherd was right—the cry was coming from a small cave about a hundred yards above us.

"He fixed his eyes on the entrance of the cave. And then He did something I'll never forget—He whistled for the wounded sheep. O how I love that sound! I've only heard it a few times in my life, but it may be more beautiful than anything else I've heard in all of God's Country. …

"Well, we both waited, holding our breath. We wondered if he was even able to walk. Then we saw him. You could tell he was sick. He walked very slowly, with his head hung towards the ground. But in the light of that sunset he still looked beautiful, and we both knew it."

Bertram's voice cracked with emotion, and he had to stop. Sherman trembled slightly. He was beginning to understand why his father loved Uncle Billy so much.

"Well," Bertram continued, "the Shepherd real-ized that Billy hadn't seen Him. So He whistled again, this time holding up His staff to catch his attention. And that's when it happened. Even from where we stood, we could see the terror on Billy's face. It wasn't the whistle that scared him—it was something about that staff. When he saw the staff he shrank back in fear, and disappeared again into the cave.

"I remember how slowly the Shepherd lowered His staff, and how He stared at it for a long time. I had never seen such a look in His eyes.

"He knelt beside me and stroked my head, just as if I were a little lamb. He spoke in a trembling voice.

"'Bertram,' He said, 'do you see this staff?'

"I nodded."

"'This wooden stick is a comfort to you and your brothers and sisters, and to all the flock; but not to the little ram in that cave. The worthless shepherds have used their staffs to hurt him. So when he sees

My shepherd's stick, he runs away from Me.' He stopped and looked up again towards the cave.

"'Bertram, I want you to go up there and invite that wounded sheep to join our flock. He's heard My call, and in his heart he wants to come. But he's afraid. He needs a friend to help him.'"

Then Sherman interrupted his father's story. "Were you scared?" he asked.

"You bet I was scared!" answered Bertram. "I knew that a cornered ram, even a sick one, could be dangerous. What's more, I had no idea what I should say. But the truth is, deep down I really wanted to go. From the moment I saw him, I liked Billy. I wanted to get to know him."

Bertram paused, reflecting on the many years he had enjoyed Billy's friendship. How good God had been to give him such a friend, a friend who was now closer than a brother. Tears of gratitude filled his eyes.

"But Father," Sherman asked with quiet urgency, "what did you say to Uncle Billy to get him to come with you?"

Bertram thought for a moment. "Funny, I can't exactly remember. I climbed up there, and just started talking to him at the mouth of the cave. Pretty soon, I knew it was okay to go in, and before long I was sitting beside him. I told him everything I could about the Shepherd's love and goodness. I could tell he really wanted to believe."

"So he came with you?" asked Sherman.

"No, that was the frustrating part. He wanted to believe me, and once or twice he even tried to get up. But in the end his fears always won out, and he'd lie back down on the ground. That really bothered me—how he kept lying back down."

Sherman could hardly believe what he was hearing. Again he jumped to his feet, begging his father to finish.

"So what happened to make him come?"

Bertram chuckled. "Well, the fact is, I got mad. He was listening more to his fears than he was to me. So I stood up, looked him in the eyes and said, 'Billy, in your heart you know I'm telling you the truth. Now in the name of the Good Shepherd Who sent me to get you, I command you to be brave. Stand up and follow me!'"

Bertram chuckled again. "And you know what?" he asked, glancing across the field towards where Uncle Billy lay sleeping.

"He did?" answered Sherman, his voice shaking.

"He did!" They both burst into laughter, and the

gentle echoes of their laughter filled the entire valley and rose to meet a happy, sparkling sky.

Sherman was certain now. Something great was happening. God had made *him* part of His plan for another ram's life—and he knew exactly what he had to do. Yes, he was afraid. But he was also confident. If God had so thoroughly prepared the plan, surely He would bring it to completion. Sherman had only to trust—and obey. With a look of contentment on his face, he lay down quietly beside his father.

"So?" inquired Bertram.

"So what?" answered Sherman.

"So, are you going to tell me what's going on? Why are you so excited about what happened to Uncle Billy?"

"Oh, that. Well, it's a long story, and it's getting late. If it's okay with you, I'll tell you tomorrow."

Bertram had to agree that it was late. "Very well. We'll talk about it first thing in the morning."

"Yes sir, first thing in the morning," replied Sherman, with a twinkle in his eyes.

Sherman lay down beside his father. As their gaze turned once again towards the Shepherd, a deep peace settled over them both. Bertram knew he should go, but the moment had caught him in its spell. He lay there in silence, remembering, thinking, savoring the special time alone with his son. Occasionally, he would glance over at Sherman and ponder the strange look of determination he saw in his eyes. *I wonder what's going on*, he mused. *Oh well, I'm sure to find out in the morning*. And at last he fell into a deep and dreamless sleep.

13
JOY IN THE MORNING

"Papa, Papa! Wake up!" It was a lamb, one of Bertram's youngest, nudging his father's side and bleating in his ear.

"Wake up, Papa! He's gone!"

"Who's gone?" mumbled Bertram, emerging from his sleep.

"Sherman! We've looked everywhere!"

"Sherman? Why he's right here beside …" Bertram stopped in mid-sentence. Sherman was not beside him at all. Immediately, he stood to his feet, shook himself awake and surveyed the flock.

"We've looked everywhere, Papa. We didn't want to wake you up, and Mama thought *we* could find him. But we've looked for two hours now, and so has Uncle Billy!"

Bertram stared at the ground and shook his head. "Oh no, not again," he said in a tired voice.

Then Uncle Billy appeared at his side and rubbed him affectionately. "Don't worry, Bertram, we'll find him."

"Have you told the Shepherd?"

"No, we thought you should do that … though I'm sure He already knows."

Fear invaded Bertram's heart. *Surely he couldn't have gone back to Sin Mountain. Surely after all that happened yesterday.* … But Bertram caught himself. This was no time to speculate. The first thing, the most important thing, was to find Sherman.

Bertram scanned the perimeter of the meadow. Soon he spotted the Shepherd sitting alone on a large rock, gazing intently towards the wilderness. Bertram began the long, difficult walk towards his Master.

He soon found, however, that he didn't walk alone. One by one the other sheep joined him. First came the older rams, noiselessly falling in step at his side. Then came the ewes, walking close behind their mates. And then, the lambs—most of whom understood little of what was going on, but who sensed the seriousness of the moment and remained subdued. A few of the older lambs, however, understood. These were the ones who looked up to Sherman as their friend and leader. The sound of their crying, though not loud, was heard by all.

As they drew near, the Shepherd heard them and

turned around. A smile spread across His face as the flock stopped and gathered itself into a tight little ball. Bertram, with Eunice at his side, stepped forward to speak. But the Shepherd spoke first.

"Children, you are beautiful this morning — more than you realize. I can see your love for Sherman, and it pleases Me very much."

The flock fell silent. The little ones were amazed that the Shepherd already knew about Sherman. Bertram exchanged glances with Billy. They were amazed — but not surprised.

Looking at Eunice and the weeping lambs, the Shepherd said gently, "Let's not listen to our fears. I'm confident that Sherman will be back soon. In fact, I'm waiting for him." The Shepherd paused, surveying the flock with evident delight. "And anyone who wants to, may wait for him with Me."

The Shepherd stroked the heads of a few sheep, then he turned around and sat down again. His twinkling eyes were fastened expectantly on the wide wilderness that spread before Him.

I wish He would go after him, said Bertram to himself. Uncle Billy was thinking the same thing. But both knew better than to speak such thoughts. They had learned that the Shepherd's ways were not their own, and that His ways always worked out best. It was a lesson to be learned over and over again.

The flock lay down in a circle behind the Shepherd. They felt it a great privilege to share in His vigil, so each tried to do his part. The rams carefully searched the horizon; the ewes whispered encouragements to one other; the lambs nuzzled their mothers reassuringly. The air was charged with suspense. Everyone knew that something important was going to happen. Hours passed, but no one dared move.

Then, as the morning sun reached its height, the Shepherd rose. He shaded his eyes with His right hand and peered intently for a full minute in the direction of Sin Mountain. A hush came over the flock.

Quickly the Shepherd jumped onto a high rock. Again He peered across the desert. Very slowly He lowered His hand. And then, just as slowly, He lowered His head.

For an endless moment the flock stared at Him. Many, especially the younger ones, were afraid. Was the Shepherd sad? Was something terrible happening? But Bertram and the older rams understood, for they had seen it before — not often, but often enough to know. So they too lowered their heads. For they knew their Master was praying—praying for joy, and giving thanks to God.

The Shepherd turned and faced the flock. "Children," He said, smiling broadly and wiping a tear from His eye with the palm of His hand, "gather round. I want to show you a great sight. Now look over there," He said, pointing. "Over towards that grove …"

The sheep quickly formed two long lines, one to their Master's right, the other to His left. Eunice, Bertram, and Billy took a few steps forward. As one body, they strained their eyes and searched among the shadows of the grove.

Several moments passed.

"See anything?" asked Billy, breaking the silence.

"No, not yet," said the weary Bertram.

"How about you, Eunice?"

"Well …," she answered cautiously "… over there, in the shade of that grove … I think …" Eunice's voice trailed off. She took a small step forward, then froze. Alert and upright, grave and dignified, she looked more like a statue than a living sheep. She was in her glory. Bertram saw it and trembled. So did the flock. The flock was proud, anxious, and strangely joyful. Everyone watched her to see what would happen next.

Suddenly, Eunice shook her head in amazement. Bertram watched as a smile quietly crept across her face. Slowly she turned towards Bertram. "It's Sherman. And it would appear," she said, grinning at Billy, "that God has given him a friend."

Once again the two rams glanced across the wilderness. But this time they saw something. At first it looked like two specks — one salt, and the other pepper, bouncing along. They shook their heads, squinted, and looked again.

"There's … there's two of them, Billy."

"I see them. … But is it really Sherman?"

A long moment passed before Bertram could answer his friend's question. Finally, Bertram was sure. Turning slowly, he looked affectionately into Billy's eyes. "Yes, Billy … It is Sherman. … And he's bringing a little black ram with him."

The two rams stared at each other in amazement, searching each other's eyes for understanding. But there was really no way to understand—only to receive—and to gratefully enjoy what God had done.

Bertram drew alongside Eunice and gave her a loving rub. And while they were side by side, he smilingly addressed the rest of the flock.

"Brothers and sisters, it's Sherman … Sherman and a new friend — a little black ram we've never met before."

The whole flock erupted with joyful baahh-ing and bleating. Dust filled the air, as each one rushed forward to congratulate Bertram and Eunice with a rub. Everyone now understood why Sherman had disappeared. The Shepherd had sent him to bring a new sheep back to the flock. He had done it — and he had done it well.

The pair of young rams drew closer and closer. Then, about a hundred yards away, they stopped. Silence fell as the Shepherd slowly strode forward to meet them.

Everyone could tell this was no easy moment for the little black sheep. Though Sherman stood right at his side, trying to encourage him, he just couldn't seem to lift up his head. And when at last he dar-ingly glanced at the approaching Shepherd, his legs began to wobble and his body began to sink.

Yes, Dudley appeared about to collapse, and probably would have, had Sherman not bumped him sternly with his rear end. It didn't hurt Dudley, but it did seem to rekindle his determination to be brave.

When at last the Shepherd reached the two rams, He stood for a moment looking thoughtfully at them. Then, with quiet decisiveness He squatted, slowly brought His face near Dudley's, and whis-pered something in his ear. No one in the flock heard what He said, but the effect of His words was soon evident to all. Dudley's tail began to fan the air madly, his back straightened and his legs grew strong beneath him. He even lifted his head and looked — very briefly — into the Shepherd's eyes.

Suddenly, the Shepherd sprang to His feet. The welcome was over — at least for now. In a business-like manner, He took a few moments to dust off the rams with His hands. Then, with the two young sheep trotting happily at His side, He headed back towards the flock.

As the Shepherd waded into their midst, all the sheep gathered excitedly around the trio. Those who could, gave Dudley a hearty rub; others shouted their welcomes over the backs of their neighbors. Meanwhile, the lambs gathered around Sherman, making a great commotion and begging him to tell them the whole story.

"Later," he said. "Now say hello to my friend."

"What's his name?" they whispered back.

"Well," said Sherman, "his name is—"

Before Sherman could finish his sentence, the Shepherd raised His hands and lifted His voice over the din.

"All right, all right, everybody quiet down for a moment," He shouted, smiling. And immediately the noise subsided. Everyone was eager to hear what He would say about the new sheep.

"As you can see, when Sherman was away from us, he found a new friend. Well, we've had a little talk, and it appears that Sherman's friend would like to join our flock."

A wave of excited whispers rolled through the crowd.

"And," said the Shepherd to the newcomer, "we are deeply grateful that God put this desire in your heart." Dudley was too shy to say so, but he was thankful, too.

Again, the Shepherd addressed the flock. "Life with us will be very different for our new friend, but I know you'll all keep encouraging him as he learns our ways." The Shepherd paused, pondering His next thought.

"In fact," He said, "it won't just be different — it will be altogether new." A wry smile appeared on His face. "So it seems to Me that the best way to begin a new life is to get a new name." There were more whispers as the Shepherd reached down and placed His hand on the black sheep's head.

"We've talked about it," said the Shepherd, "and decided that 'Timothy' would make an excellent name. I've known some other Timothys before, very special rams. I think the name will fit quite well."

For a second, the Shepherd appeared lost in thought, as if He were taking a long journey back through time. Then His face brightened again. Smiling, He nudged the sheep forward and said, "So let me introduce you to young Timothy, Sherman's friend ... and My friend, too."

Immediately, the whole flock broke into a loud chorus of welcomes. This time the lambs were the first to get beside the newcomer. "Hi, Tim!" said one. "Hey, Timothy!" said another—and another and another, as all gave him the traditional welcome rub.

It was a long, happy morning for Timothy, as each sheep greeted him. At first, the new name the Shepherd gave him sounded strange. But with each greeting, he got more used to it. In fact, before long it even started to "fit," just as the Shepherd said it would. So the little black ram, with amazement and gratitude, said good-bye to the old Dudley and took his new name to heart. He decided then and there to be the very best Timothy he could be.

"Children," said the Shepherd, as the last sheep greeted Timothy, "the time has come for us to return to the lowlands, and to My Father's house." It was the news they all had been waiting to hear. Immediately the flock was astir, as each sought out his family and took his proper place for the long journey home.

Timothy looked bewildered, not having a family to join. The Shepherd must have noticed, for He said, "As for you, Timothy, I have someone I'd like you to meet."

Timothy turned toward the Shepherd and saw there standing beside him a solitary black ram — his wool streaked with gray. His face had a kindly look, and Timothy liked him right away.

"Tim," said the Shepherd, "this is Billy. I want you to walk with him on the way home. He has much to teach you." The Shepherd glanced at Uncle Billy with a grin. "And who knows? Maybe he'll even tell you how he got *his* name."

"Come on," said Billy, with the eagerness of a child, "I'll show you our place. It's reserved for old-timers like me — and their friends."

Timothy, curious and thrilled, fell in at Billy's side, and they moved towards the head of the flock. The Shepherd smiled affectionately as He watched them amble along together like father and son.

Moments later, the sheep were all assembled. The older rams stood at the front. Bertram, Eunice, Billy, Timothy, and Sherman were next, surrounded by admiring little lambs. The rest of the sheep fanned out behind them in orderly columns.

Then the Shepherd appeared and took His place before them all. As usual, He scanned the entire flock, whispering the name of each sheep. When His gaze rested at last upon little Timothy, they all knew He had completed His count.

"You are very beautiful today," said the Shepherd, "… more than you realize. My Father will be so glad to see you all."

He offered a brief prayer, thanking God for His faithful care, and asking for a safe journey home. Then with happy eyes looking down at Sherman and Timothy, He cried in a loud voice for all to hear, "Follow Me!"

And He turned, and led them forth.

About the Author

Dean Davis

Born and raised in the San Francisco Bay Area, Dean graduated with a degree in Philosophy from the University of California at Santa Cruz. After several unsatisfying years on Sin Mountain, the Good Shepherd rescued him, eventually making him a pastor in Santa Rosa, CA.

Dean has often worked with children and youth, and very much enjoys telling them stories. He is currently director of *Come Let Us Reason*, a Bible teaching ministry specializing in the study of apologetics and the biblical worldview. Dean and his wife, Linda, have a little flock of their own: five children (two "rams" and three "ewes"), ages 16 to 24.